Tigers A to Z

Mark Walter

illustrated by
Tim Williams

Dedication

Special thanks to Maggie and Chris "BC" LeBato and Mr. and Mrs. Doyle "Bubba" Spell (LSU Varsity Boxer, 1955) for their knowledge and assistance with editing. Also, thanks to my wife Breane, the Walter family, and the Barker family for their continued support.

—

Tigers A to Z

Copyright © 2011 by Mark Walter

Requests for permission to make copies of any part of the work should be submitted online at info@mascotbooks.com or mailed to Mascot Books, 560 Herndon Parkway #120, Herndon, VA 20170

PRT1011A

Printed in the United States.

ISBN-13: 978-1-936319-73-2
ISBN-10: 1-936319-73-X

www.mascotbooks.com

Way to go,
You've finished the book.
Here are some fun activities,
Just take a look...

Skip Counting to Victory

In football, each touchdown with an extra point is worth 7 points, a field goal is worth 3 points, and a safety is worth 2 points. Can you count points in a football game?
Give it a try.

Count by 7's – 7, 14, 21, 28, 35, 42, 49, 56, 63, 70, 77, 84, 91...

Count by 3's – 3, 6, 9, 12, 15, 18, 21, 24, 27, 30, 33, 36, 39, 42...

Count by 2's – 2, 4, 6, 8, 10, 12, 14, 16, 18, 20, 22, 24, 26, 28...

What's the Score?

Make up math story problems for yourself, a friend, or a family member like the examples shown below. Then try to solve them.

●If a team scores two touchdowns with extra points and three field goals, how many points do they have?

7+7+3+3+3=23 points

●If the Tigers have 31 points and their opponent has 14 points, how many points are the Tigers winning by?

31 – 14 = 17 point lead

The Tigers have pulled out many last-second victories over the years, including the 2002 "Bluegrass Miracle." LSU scored on a 75 yard touchdown pass from Marcus Randall to Devery Henderson to beat Kentucky as time expired.

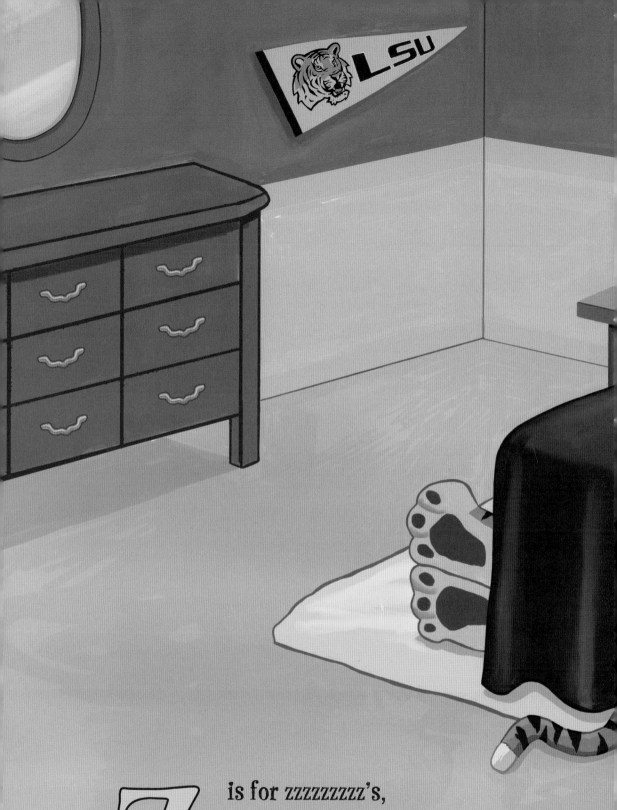

Z is for zzzzzzzz's,
You'll need sleep after you play.
Four quarters each game,
Makes for a mighty long day!

Y is for Y.A. Tittle,
Winning was his goal.
He's one of the best we've ever had,
MVP of the Cotton Bowl.

Y.A. Tittle was the MVP of the icy 1947 Cotton Bowl against rival Arkansas. He is remembered as one of LSU's great quarterbacks. LSU and Arkansas continue their rivalry with the winner taking home the Golden Boot trophy, which weighs about 200 pounds, is over 4 feet tall, and is molded out of 24-karat gold.

"THE BOOT"

 is for GEAUX,
Spelled G-E-A-U-X.
The fans cheer it loud,
In the Tiger complex.

Before, during, and after games, LSU fans greet each other with cheers of "Geaux Tigers,"
a tribute to the strong French Cajun heritage in Louisiana.

Most college football teams wear their dark jerseys for home games, but in 1958 Coach Dietzel decided that LSU would wear white jerseys at home. The team went on to win the national championship and a tradition was born.

W is for white jerseys,
Worn at home for good luck.
Since 1958,
This tradition has stuck.

V is for Victory Hill,
A gathering place for fans.
To cheer on the band, cheerleaders, and team,
Before heading into the stands.

Before each home game, thousands of fans come to see the coaches, players, cheerleaders, and Mike the Tiger as they head to Tiger Stadium with The Golden Band from Tigerland.

U

is for university,

LSU is a sight to see.

With oaks, magnolias, and the Indian Mounds,

It's a beautiful place to be.

Tim Williams

LSU's campus is known for its live oak and magnolia trees that were planted in the 1930's. It is also known for the Indian Mounds that are believed to be over 5,000 years old.

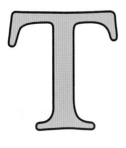 is for Tiger Bait,
SEC teams that we play.
Florida, Ole Miss, Alabama,
And others that stand in the way.

 **is for Shaquille O'Neal,**
One of the best to play the sport.
National Player of the Year,
He was a giant on the court.

Shaquille O'Neal won the 1991 Rupp Trophy as the nation's best basketball player. He was a two-time All-American and his #33 jersey was retired by LSU.

R is for receivers,
Like the star Josh Reed.
He set many offensive records,
With his dazzling speed.

Josh Reed won the 2001
Biletnikoff Award given to
the nation's best receiver.

Q is for quarterbacks,
Like Rabb, Mauck, and Flynn.
Each led our Tigers,
To a national championship win.

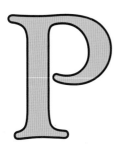

P is for Pettit,
He made the Final Four.
As a great basketball player,
He's forever in Tiger lore.

Bob Pettit, Jr. led the Tigers to their first Final Four appearance in 1953. His #50 jersey has been retired by LSU. Other Tiger basketball greats include Howard Carter (1979-1983), Don Redden (1982-1986), Stromile Swift (1998-2000), Brandon Bass (2003-2005), and Glen Davis (2004-2007).

Running backs Joseph Addai (2002-2005) and Jacob Hester (2004-2007) helped lead the Tigers to the 2003 and 2007 national championships, respectively. Charles Scott (2006-2009) also was a member of the 2007 national championship team and helped lead the Tiger rushing attack during his time at LSU.

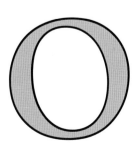

is for offense,
Guys like Hester, Scott, and Addai.
When carrying the ball,
These guys could really fly.

N is for national champs,
The prize for winning it all.
The Tigers have won many,
By playing really great ball.

LSU won football national championships in 1958, 2003, 2007, _____, _____.
The Tigers won baseball national championships in 1991, 1993, 1996, 1997, 2000, 2009, _____, _____.
The Tigers were basketball national champions in 1935, _____, _____.

LSU has become one of the best baseball programs in the country due, in part, to legendary coach Skip Bertman (5 national championships) and players like pitcher Ben McDonald, the 1989 National Player of the Year. Other Tiger greats include College World Series Most Outstanding Players Gary Hymel (1991), Todd Walker (1993), Brandon Larson (1997), Trey Hodges (2000), and Jared Mitchell (2009).

Tim Williams

is for Ben McDonald,
1989 Player of the Year.
He pitched his way to greatness,
On the mound he had no fear.

GUS TINSLEY

JERRY STOVALL

JIM TAYLOR

LSU Legends

LSU Legend

LSU Legends

Jerry Stovall, an All-American running back in 1962, later became head coach (1980-1983). Gaynell "Gus" Tinsley, an All-American in 1935 and 1936, also became head coach (1948-1954). Jim Taylor was an All-American in 1957. Other Tiger legends include Ken Kavanaugh (1937-1939), Doc Fenton (1907-1909), and Abe Mickal (1933-1935).

L is for legends,
Great players from the past.
Like Stovall, Tinsley, and Taylor,
They made memories that last.

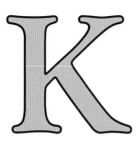 **K** is for Kevin Faulk,
One of our best running backs.
Feared by opposing players,
He led the LSU rushing attack.

Kevin Faulk (1995-1998), one of the best running backs in Tiger history, holds many offensive records at LSU. These include most career rushing yards (4,557), most career all purpose yards (6,833), and most rushing touchdowns in a game (5).

J is for jambalaya,
A tasty Cajun cuisine.
Like crawfish, shrimp, and gumbo,
They are a tailgater's dream.

I

is for intensity,
This defense delivers big hits.
In the year 1958,
They were called the Chinese Bandits.

In 1958, Coach Dietzel named his 2nd string defense the Chinese Bandits. The Bandits helped lead the team to the national championship and the name stuck.
Some defensive greats over the years include Ronnie Estay (1969-1971), Mike Williams (1972-1974), Marcus Spears (2001-2004), LaRon Landry (2003-2006), Glenn Dorsey (2004-2007), and Patrick Peterson (2008-2010).

Billy Cannon was an All-American halfback in 1958 and 1959. He won the Heisman Trophy in 1959.

H is for the Heisman Trophy,
The prize for being the best.
In '59 the great Billy Cannon,
Was better than all the rest.

The Golden Girls first performed on the field with the band in 1959. This group of dancers is a well-recognized part of football Saturdays and other campus events.

G is for our Golden Girls,
LSU's famous dance line.
Their performance is a sight to see,
A Tiger tradition since '59.

The 325-member LSU Marching Band, called "The Golden Band from Tigerland," is known for its fabulous pregame show and plays the "First Down Cheer" each time the Tigers earn a first down.

F is for the First Down Cheer,
Led by our Golden Band.
When they play the cheer "Geaux Tigers,"
It's heard across the land.

E is for excellence,
Perfect in '58.
Led by Coach Dietzel,
This team was truly great.

Paul Dietzel coached LSU from 1955-1961.
In 1958 the Tigers went 11-0 and were
named national champions.

Tiger Stadium holds over 92,000 fans and is known as "Death Valley." In the 1988 game against Auburn, LSU fans cheered so loud after a game-winning touchdown pass from Tommy Hodson to Eddie Fuller on 4th down that the noise registered as an earthquake.

D

is for Death Valley,
With the best fans in the States.
In '88 we cheered so loudly,
It caused a real earthquake.

C is for Casanova,
A three-time All-American.
He did it all for LSU,
He's in the heart of every fan.

While at LSU from 1969-1971, Tommy Casanova played running back, defensive back, kick returner, and punt returner. He was a three-time All-American and is remembered as one of the best players in Tiger football history.

Baton Rouge is the state capital of Louisiana and is also the location of Louisiana State University. LSU is the largest university in the state.

B is for Baton Rouge,
The hometown of our team.
Playing for LSU,
Is every Tiger fan's dream.

LSU plays basketball in the PMAC (Pete Maravich Assembly Center). Pete Maravich, a three-time All-American, won the 1970 Naismith Award given to the nation's best basketball player.

is for Alex Box Stadium,
Where the baseball Tigers compete.
And for the Assembly Center,
The PMAC's named for "Pistol Pete."

GERRY LANE CHAMPIONSHIP PLAZA

The original Alex Box Stadium was home to Tiger baseball from 1938-2008. LSU's great tradition of winning and its record-setting crowds are now carried on in the new Alex Box Stadium, which opened in 2009 and can seat 10,150 fans.

Young Tiger fans gather 'round,
Your learning tool has now been found.
You'll learn LSU facts from A to Z,
And become a Tiger just like me.

Hidden within each picture,
Is Mike the Tiger our mascot.
You can find him if you try,
Go ahead and give it a shot!

For
Finn
(finally)

Finn's Mustache

Written and Illustrated by
Timothy Stewart

Author's Note

Market research has shown that tracing each of the mustaches in this book with your finger while adding your own creative sound effects greatly enhances the reading experience.

You can try saying, "Whoop, whoop" or "Ka-kaw, ka-kaw."

Go ahead, give it a try.

Practice on this soup-strainer.

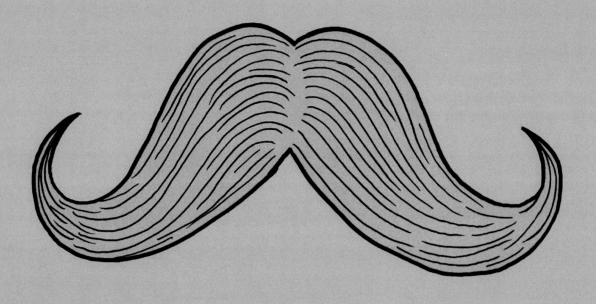

See, wasn't that amazing?

Enjoy!

Almost everyone in Finn's family had a mustache.

His uncles
had mustaches.

The dog had a mustache.

The cats had mustaches.

The fish had a mustache.

Even Granny had a mustache.

Finn did not have a mustache, and this made him sad.

"How did you get your mustache, Uncle Pinniped?" asked Finn.

"I grew this sardine-scaler while studying marine mammals," said Uncle Pinniped. "Why do you ask?"

"Where did you get your mustache, Granny?"

"I don't have a mustache," growled Granny.

Finn realized every mustache had a story.

"I must go and find my mustache," said Finn.

He tried a caterpillar, but it just crawled off and left him itchy.

He tried many things...

Finn slouched on the couch.

"Don't worry, son," said Dad, "your 'stache will grow when you get older."

And Dad was right.

Made in the USA
San Bernardino, CA
21 June 2018